To Sam and the B's —Maureen

For Tom. The last guy we know who plays hockey! —Mark

THIS IS A BORZOI BOOK PUBLISHED BY ALFRED A. KNOPF

Visit us on the Web! rhcbooks.com

Educators and librarians, for a variety of teaching tools, visit us at RHTeachersLibrarians.com

Library of Congress Cataloging-in-Publication Data is available upon request.

ISBN 978-1-5247-1451-2 (trade) — ISBN 978-1-5247-1452-9 (lib. bdg.) — ISBN 978-1-5247-1453-6 (ebook)

The text of this book is set in Meta Pro point 16.

The illustrations were created using pencil, paper, and Photoshop utilizing various digital brushes.

Book design by Sarah Hokanson

MANUFACTURED IN CHINA October 2020 10 9 8 7 6 5 4 3 2 1 First Edition

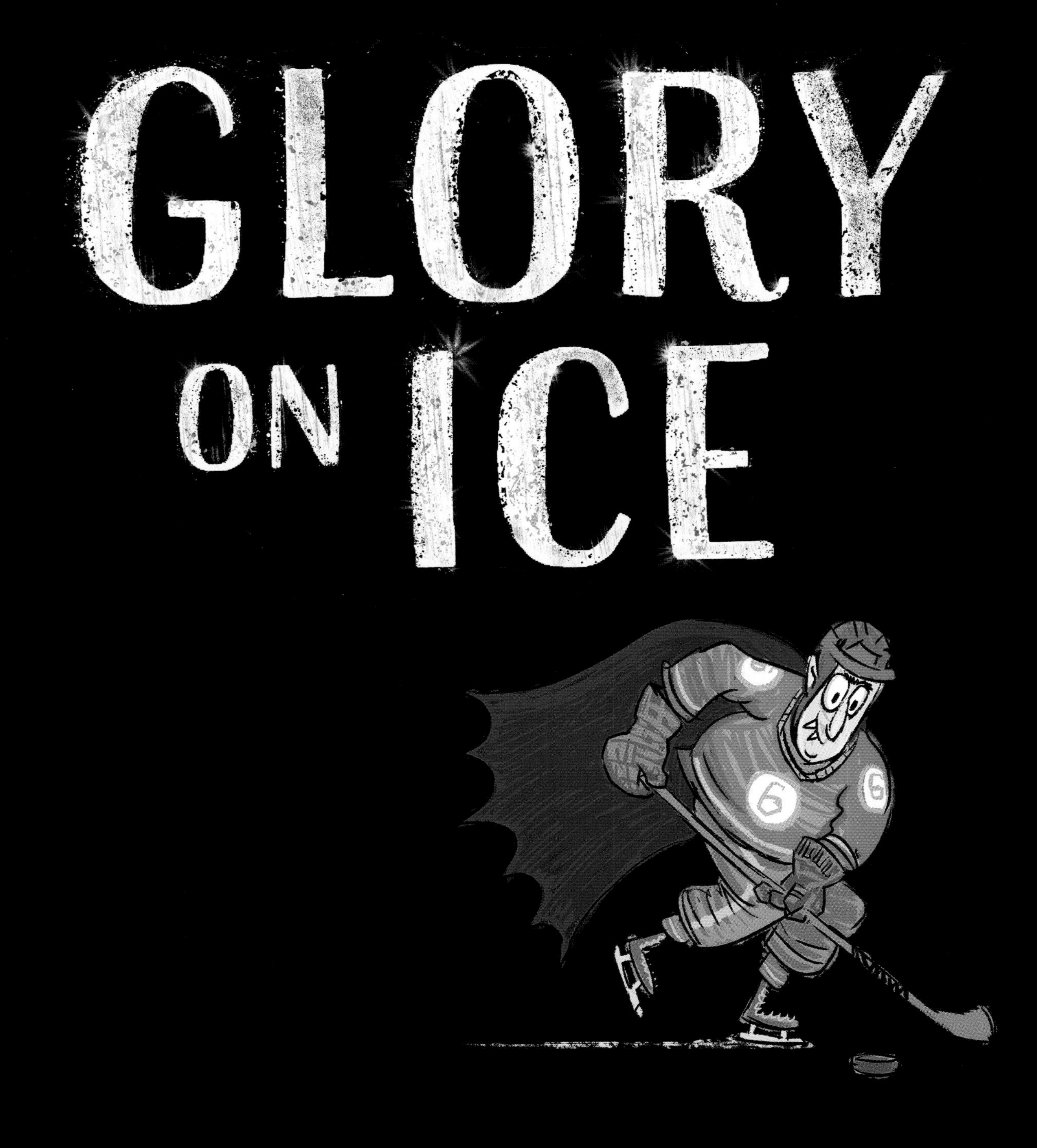

by Maureen Fergus illustrated by Mark Fearing

Alfred A. Knopf  New York

In some ways, Vlad had it all.

He had a lovely home.

He had more money than he knew what to do with.

He hadn't aged a day in eight hundred years.

But after centuries of doing the same old thing, Vlad was feeling a bit bored.

It was time to find a new hobby.

So Vlad strolled down to the local community center to check out what kinds of activities they offered.

Dancing was fun, but Vlad wasn't sure he had the rhythm for it.

Scrapbooking was creative, but Vlad wasn't sure he had the patience for it.

Water aerobics was good exercise, but Vlad wasn't sure he had the legs for it.

Just as Vlad was starting to worry that he was never going to find the perfect activity, he walked past the hockey registration desk.

"This year, we're going to pound those Hounds," said one kid.

"We're going to crush them," said another.
"We're going to destroy them!" shouted a third.

Pounding? Crushing? Destroying?
Vlad signed up on the spot.

The following day, Vlad headed over to the sports store and told the saleswoman he wanted the best hockey equipment that treasure plundered from ancient gravesites could buy.

He was extremely impressed by the prompt service he received.

For the next week, Vlad practiced putting on his equipment.

He read hockey books and watched hockey games.

He dreamed of playing for Team Transylvania in the gold medal match at the next Olympics.

When the day of his first practice finally arrived, Vlad excitedly entered his assigned dressing room, only to be hit by a stench so revolting that he thought his new teammates must surely be overgrown ogres!

Then he saw that they were just little human beings.

"Amazing!" thought Vlad.

After introducing himself to everyone, Vlad put on his equipment and sat patiently while one of the moms tightened his skates for him.

Then, eager to hit the ice for the very first time, he followed the others out to the rink, bounded through the gate, and . . .

. . . fell flat on his backside.

Vlad was baffled.

He had the best equipment! He'd watched people skate on TV! He'd dreamed of glory on ice!

Plus, he was an immortal creature who possessed some pretty nifty powers!

After careful consideration, Vlad concluded that his powers did not include the power to skate.

If he wanted to learn how to play hockey, he was going to have to do it the hard way.

And so, since Vlad had come to love hockey even more than he loved chasing after terrified mortals, he unsteadily stood up and got to work.

In the weeks that followed, Vlad practiced skating forward and backward, turning and stopping, passing and shooting.

Some days, it seemed like he was really improving!

Other days, it was like he'd never played before in his life.

Vlad often felt embarrassed by how much better everyone else was. But his teammates were so supportive, and he loved the game so much, that he never gave up.

By the day of his team's first regular season game against the Hounds, Vlad could sometimes skate almost all the way across the rink without losing the puck, tripping, or running into someone.

He was ready for anything!

At least, he *thought* he was ready for anything.

Vlad's first instinct when he saw the hulking, heckling Hounds was to fly over and destroy every last one of them.

However, since he was pretty sure that kind of behavior would earn him a three-game suspension, he just got out there and gave it everything he had.

And if Vlad wasn't the fastest player, he was certainly the hardest-working.

And if he wasn't the strongest player, he was unquestionably the most courageous.

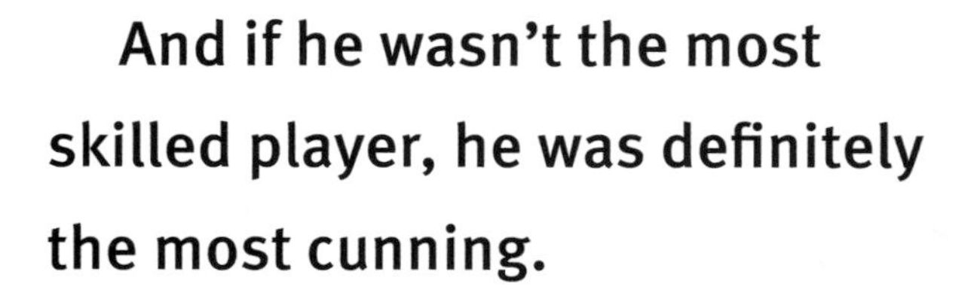

And if he wasn't the most skilled player, he was definitely the most cunning.

He spent a great deal of
time in the penalty box.

By the time the game was over, Vlad was more exhausted than he'd been in his entire immortal existence.

And even though he and his team had done their best, they ended up losing fifty-seven to nothing.

"Don't worry, Vlad," said his teammates. "With a little more practice, we'll beat them for sure!"

Vlad wasn't worried.

Win or lose, he knew they were in it together.

And for a hockey-playing vampire who'd spent centuries alone, that was the best feeling in the world.